Jogger's Big Adventure

You can read more stories about the gang from Buffin Street by collecting the rest of the series.

For complete list, look at the back of the book.

Jogger's
Big
Adventure

Francesca Simon

Illustrated by Emily Bolam

Orion
Children's Books

Jogger's Big Adventure first appeared in *Miaow Miaow Bow Wow*
first published in Great Britain in 2000
by Orion Children's Books
This edition first published in Great Britain in 2012
by Orion Children's Books
a division of the Orion Publishing Group Ltd
Orion House
5 Upper St Martin's Lane
London WC2H 9EA
An Hachette UK Company

1 3 5 7 9 10 8 6 4 2

Printed in China

The Orion Publishing Group's policy is to use papers that are natural,
renewable and recyclable products made from wood grown in sustainable forests.
The logging and manufacturing processes are expected to conform
to the environmental regulations of the country of origin.

www.orionbooks.co.uk

For Josh

Hello from everyone

Millie

Flick

Rustle rustle

Jogger

Growl

Sour Puss

Miaow

Lola

Woof

Honey

Snuffle
snuffle

Lily

Caw Caw

Do-Re-Mi

Bow wow

Prince

Miaow

Joey

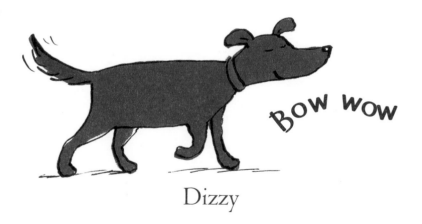

Bow wow

Dizzy

Miaow

Kit

Squeak   Squeak

Doris   Boris

Woof

Fang

Welcome to Buffin Street!

Come and join all the Buffin Street
dogs, cats, rabbits, puppies and parrots,
and find out what *really* goes on when
their people are out of sight…

Wheeee!

thought Jogger the hamster,
running round and round
in his wheel.
Now what shall I do?

He'd played in his sand bowl,
tidied his bedding, raced
in his wheel, and filled
his hoard with food.
He'd even cleaned his face.

Ah! He'd gnaw on his cage door.
That was always good fun.

Jogger scampered about in
the wood shavings and started
to chew on the bars.

Nibble
Gnaw

Nibble
Gnaw

Nibble
Gnaw

Then a strange thing happened.
The door started to move.

SF/2204003

Jogger pushed.
The door opened more.
He pushed, and wriggled through.
Thud!

Jogger landed on the ground.
Oh my!

This had never happened to him
before when he'd gnawed on the door.

What an adventure!

He'd always wondered what
the world was like outside his cage.
Now he'd find out.

Bounce

Bounce

Bounce

Jogger plopped down some
stairs, then found himself in a
gigantic passageway.
He pitter-pattered along it, then
darted through a doorway.

What a fascinating place!

He explored behind the
chest of drawers.

He nibbled on a book.

He swung on the duvet.

He tried climbing up a chair.

"Miaow!
Miaow!"

Jogger peeped out from
behind the chair leg.

Oh no!

It was that nasty Sour Puss, who
always liked sitting on top of his cage
and staring at him with
a hungry look in her slitty eyes.

Jogger saw her sniff the air.
And Jogger did not like
the way she sniffed.

Hide!

he thought, and darted
under the bed.

Sour Puss turned and
lunged at him.

Bang!

She whacked her head on the bed.
She staggered about for a moment,
feeling rather dizzy.

"Jogger! Come out,
come out wherever you are!"
hissed Sour Puss.

No way,
thought Jogger.

Suddenly two horrible
green eyes blazed
straight at him.

"I know you're under there," said Sour Puss. "I'll be glad to guide you back to your cage."

I don't think so, thought Jogger.

Zip!

Jogger darted
behind the bedpost.

Pounce!

Smash!

Sour Puss hit her head
on the post.

"Eeowwww!"

she squealed,
her head throbbing.

I've got to get away, thought
Jogger, his heart beating fast.

He darted out of the room,
chased by Sour Puss.

He escaped into the toilet
and hid behind the loo.

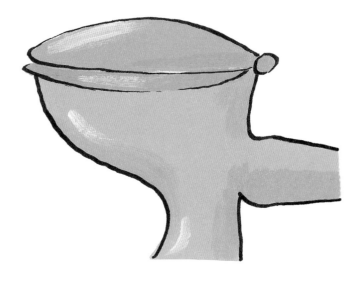

Sour Puss scurried in
after him.

"Aha!" said Sour Puss,
jumping on the loo.

Crash!

The loo seat smashed
down on Sour Puss.

"Owwww!"
she yowled.

Tee hee,

thought Jogger, scampering
away into the kitchen.
He could outsmart
that stupid cat any day.

"I'll get you!"
snarled Sour Puss,
staggering after him.

Clunk!

The kitchen door swung
shut in her face.

"Eoowwwww!"

Jogger looked round and sighed.
Wow, that was close, he thought,
his heart pounding.

Safe at last.

Sour Puss couldn't get him now. He'd
have a sniff round,
then find his way back home.

Suddenly the cat flap
started to move.

"Gotcha!"
miaowed Sour Puss,
wriggling through the flap.

Jogger froze.

"Eeeeeeee!"

he squeaked.

Sour Puss was
in the room.

"Help!"

Sour Puss got ready to leap.

He was **dead.**

Goodbye world!

Suddenly a giant hand
scooped him up.
"Jogger, what are you doing here?"

"Phew."

Safely back in his cage, Jogger
buried himself in the bedding.
He'd had enough adventures —
for that day, anyway.

Eeeek
follow me

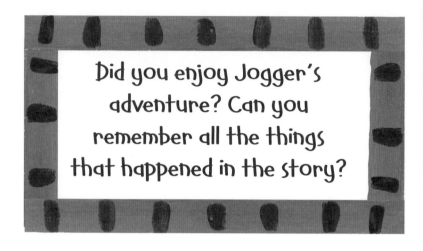

Did you enjoy Jogger's adventure? Can you remember all the things that happened in the story?

What is Jogger doing when his cage door swings open?

What does Jogger think of the outside world?

Where does Jogger explore first?

What is Jogger doing when he spots
Sour Puss?

Where does Jogger hide from Sour
Puss first?

Where does Jogger hide from Sour
Puss next?

What happens when Sour Puss jumps
on the loo?

How does Jogger make his lucky escape?

For more adventures with the
Buffin Street Gang, look out for
the other books in the series.

Meet
the Gang

Rampage
in Prince's
Garden

Yum Yum

Miaow
Miaow
Bow Wow

The Haunted House of Buffin Street

Look at Me